My Weird School Daze #8

Miss Laney Is Zany!

Dan Gutman

Pictures by
Jim Paillot

HARPER
An Imprint of HarperCollinsPublishers

To Emma

Thanks to Nicole Abbatemarco, Naomi Gerstenblith, Janet Goodman, Chris Horwitz, Helen Pires

Library of Congress Cataloging-in-Publication Data is available.

ISBN 978-0-06-155417-9 (lib. bdg.) – ISBN 978-0-06-155415-5 (pbk.)

Typography by Joel Tippie

19 20 BRR 30 29 28 27 26 25

❖

First Edition

Contents

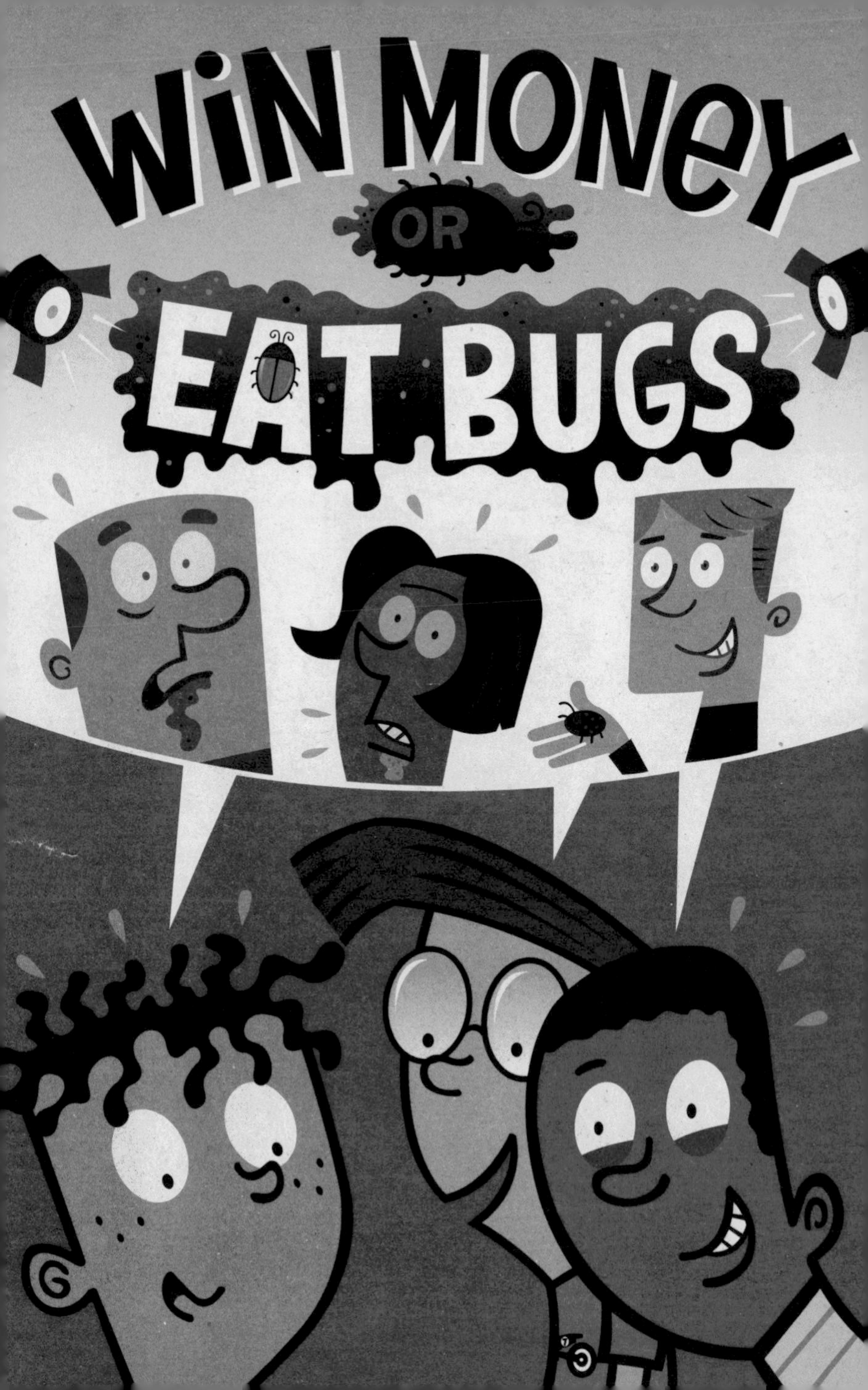
WIN MONEY
OR
EAT BUGS

Bad News

My name is A.J. and I hate school.

But I have to go anyway. My friend Billy who lives around the corner told me that if you don't go to school, they throw you in jail. Then you have to wear one of those striped uniforms and drag around a ball and chain.

1

I go to Ella Mentry School, and my teacher is Mr. Granite, who is from another planet. It was Monday morning, and the girls were talking about silly girl stuff, like how many stuffed animals they have on their beds. Me and the guys were talking about important guy stuff, like my favorite TV show—*Win Money or Eat Bugs*.

It's a cool show. You have to answer a bunch of questions. If you get them right, you win money. If you get them wrong, you have to eat bugs. So *Win Money or Eat Bugs* has the perfect name. Some people win money. But most people have to eat bugs. That show is hilarious.

After we put our backpacks into our cubbies, the school secretary, Mrs. Patty, made an announcement over the loud-speaker. We had to go to the all-purpose room for a surprise assembly.

"Why are we having an assembly?" asked Andrea Young, this annoying girl in my class with curly brown hair.

"Beats me," said her crybaby friend Emily.

Everybody was in the all-purpose room. Miss Lazar, the custodian. Ms. LaGrange, the lunch lady. Even Mr. Tony, who runs the after-school program, was there. I could tell it wasn't a normal assembly. We were all buzzing about what was up.*

We had to sit crisscross applesauce.

---

* But not like when a machine is buzzing. If people made buzzing noises like machines, it would be weird.

Finally our principal, Mr. Klutz, got up on the stage. He has no hair at all. I mean *none*. They should use his head to bounce laser beams around the world. Mr. Klutz held up his hand and made a peace sign, which means "shut up."

"I have bad news," Mr. Klutz said.

"Mr. Klutz has a bad nose," I whispered to my friend Michael, who never ties his shoes.

"As you probably heard from your parents," Mr. Klutz told us, "the economy is in bad shape. We have been trying to save money ever since our budget was cut. But last night I got a call from the Board of Education. I'm sorry to tell you this, but . . . Ella Mentry School will be closing in June."

Everybody laughed. Mr. Klutz is so funny!

"It's not a joke," he added.

Suddenly, it was quiet in the all-purpose room. You could hear a pin drop.*

"Do you mean the school will close for a few weeks?" asked Mr. Granite.

"No," Mr. Klutz replied. "The school is closing *forever.*"

"Forever?"

"Forever."

---

* That is, if somebody actually dropped a pin. But who carries pins around with them anyway? That would be a weird thing to do. Unless you really like to sew stuff, I guess.

I looked at Michael. Michael looked at Ryan. Ryan looked at Neil, who we call the nude kid even though he wears clothes. Then we all jumped out of our seats at the same time.

"Yeah!" me and the guys shouted. "No more school!"

"You'll still have to go to school," Mr. Klutz told us. "You'll just have to go to *another* school. A school that's farther away."

Oh. Bummer in the summer!

"Will the teachers be fired?" asked Mr. Granite.

"I'm afraid so," Mr. Klutz said. "The whole staff will lose their jobs. And that includes me. We're all in the same boat."

I looked around. I didn't see a boat any-
where.

"What do boats have to do with it?" I
asked.

"That means we're all in this *together*,
Arlo," whispered Andrea. She calls me by
my real name because she knows I don't
like it.

"There will be more budget cuts
between now and June," Mr. Klutz said.
"So we'll all have to tighten our belts.
Does anybody have any questions?"

"What if you don't wear a belt?" I
asked.

"Tightening our belts means we have

to save money, dumbhead," Andrea whispered, rolling her eyes.

"Your face needs to save money," I told her.

I hate Andrea.

"Isn't there anything we can do?" asked Mr. Granite.

"I'm afraid not," Mr. Klutz said. "It will cost a million dollars to keep the school open."

"WOW," everybody said, which is "MOM" upside down. We all started buzzing again. The teachers looked worried. A few first graders started crying.

It was the saddest day in the history of the world.

The Mystery of the Girls' Bathroom

When we got back to our classroom, two big guys wearing overalls were carrying out Mr. Granite's desk.

"Hey, what are you doing?" Mr. Granite shouted.

"Sorry, bud," one of the guys said. "Budget cuts."

Mr. Granite was mad because he didn't

have a desk
anymore. But
he still had to
teach us math.
I raised my hand
to ask a question,
and Mr. Granite said it had to be about
math.

"How many dollars is a million?" I asked.

"Well, let's say you have one dollar," Mr. Granite told me, "and then you get a million more dollars. Then you'd have a million dollars."

That made sense.

"No you wouldn't," said Andrea. "You'd have a million and *one* dollars."

Andrea had a big smile on her face, like she was all proud of herself. Why can't a million dollars fall on her head? A million dollars in *coins*.

We were all sad about the school closing down. Mr. Granite wasn't in the mood to teach, and nobody was in the mood to learn anything. Not even Andrea.

Luckily, we have art class on Mondays. We walked a million hundred miles to the art room. Ms. Hannah, the art teacher, was cutting a piece of cardboard into a bunch of tiny little squares.

"What are we doing in art today?" asked Emily.

"Because of the budget cuts, I can only use one sheet of cardboard for the whole class," said Ms. Hannah. "So today we're going to make postage stamps."

"Postage stamps?" we all asked.

"We all have to do our part to save money," she said.

I made a little frowny face on my stamp,

and there wasn't room to draw anything else. Making postage stamps in art class is lame.

When we got back to Mr. Granite's room, Mrs. Patty made an announcement over the loudspeaker.

"A.J., please report to the girls' bathroom."

What?! I thought I was gonna die.

Ryan, Michael, and Neil thought it was hilarious. They were falling off their chairs.

"A.J. has to go to the girls' bathroom," Michael said. "He must be a girl!"

"There must be some mistake," Mr. Granite said.

"I'm not going to the girls' bathroom,"
I announced. "What if there are girls in
there?"

"Of *course* there will be girls in there,"
Andrea said. "It's the girls'—"

She didn't have the chance to finish her
sentence because Mrs. Patty made another
announcement.

"Ryan, please report to the girls' bathroom."

What?!

"I'm not going to—"

Ryan didn't have the chance to finish
his sentence because Mrs. Patty made
another announcement.

"Andrea, please report to the girls'

bathroom."

What?!

And then Mrs. Patty made *another* announcement.

"Emily, please report to the girls' bathroom."

"I guess the four of you should go to the girls' bathroom," Mr. Granite told us.

He gave me, Ryan, Andrea, and Emily passes; and we walked down the hall to the girls' bathroom.

"You open the door," I told Andrea. "You're a girl."

Andrea put her hand on the doorknob.

Andrea turned the doorknob.

She pulled open the door.

16

And you'll never believe in a million hundred years what we saw in there.

I'm not gonna tell you.

Okay, okay, I'll tell you. But you have to read the next chapter first. So nah-nah-nah boo-boo on you!

Miss Laney Is Weird

In the middle of the girls' bathroom was a lady with dark hair. She was sitting behind a desk—Mr. Granite's desk.

"Come on in!" the lady said excitedly. She sounded like one of those game show hosts on TV.

"Who are you?" asked Andrea.

"I'm Miss Laney, the new speech teacher," the lady said. "I'm *soooooo* glad you could join me today!"

Miss Laney is *way* too enthusiastic about stuff.

I always wondered what was in the girls' bathroom. I looked around. There were three stalls against the wall but no urinals. On the walls were a bunch of posters with pictures of TV stars.

Girls' bathrooms are weird.

"Why is your office in the bathroom?" asked Emily.

"Because of budget cuts, they couldn't afford to give me a regular office," Miss Laney told us. "But a bathroom is perfect for speech class. This room has really good acoustics."

"I don't see any good cue sticks," I said. "My uncle has a pool table in his basement, and he's got some *really* good cue sticks."

"Not 'cue sticks,' dumbhead!" Andrea said, rolling her eyes. "'Acoustics'!"

It sounded a lot like "a cue stick" to me.

"Do you know what the word 'acoustics' means?" Miss Laney asked.

"Yes!" Andrea said, "acoustics is the science of sound."

"Very good, Andrea!" Miss Laney said, all smiley.

Little Miss Brownnoser knows about dumb stuff like acoustics because she reads the encyclopedia for the fun of it. What is her problem?

"Wait a minute," Emily said. "If this is the speech room now, where should we go to the bathroom?"

"In your pants!" I said. Ryan cracked up.

"Starting today," Miss Laney told us, "the girls go to the bathroom in the boys' bathroom."

What?!

"If the girls go to the bathroom in the boys' bathroom, where will the boys go to the bathroom?" Ryan asked.

"Out there," Miss Laney said.

I looked out the window. There was a tree outside.

"We have to use a tree?" I asked.

"There's a porta-potty near the tree," Miss Laney said.

I stood on my tiptoes at the window and saw the porta-potty.

"I'd rather use the tree," I said.

"Yeah, can we use the tree?" asked Ryan.

"That could kill the tree, Arlo," Andrea said.

"Your face could kill a tree," I told Andrea.

"There must be some mistake, Miss Laney," Emily said. "We don't need speech class."

"Yeah," I agreed, "we already know how to talk."

"Of course you know how to talk," Miss Laney said. "But Mr. Granite told me you're having a little trouble understanding idioms, A.J."

"Oh, snap!" said Ryan. "She called you an idiot!"

"And Ryan, sometimes you have difficulty with *R* sounds," Miss Laney said. "And Emily, you have trouble pronouncing the letters *T* and *D*. And Andrea, you occasionally have trouble with grammar."

Little Miss Perfect looked all mad. I guess nobody ever told her she had anything wrong with her before.

"Speech is boring," I said.

"Yeah, we don't want to be here," said Ryan.

"I speak perfectly," Andrea insisted.

"Is that so?" asked Miss Laney. "Well, let's find out!"

That's when the weirdest thing in the history of the world happened. Miss Laney took a top hat out of the desk drawer and put it on her head.* Then she took a little boom box out of the desk and pushed a button on it. Thumping music came out of the boom box. Miss Laney started to dance around. The lights in the bathroom started flashing on and off.

Next, a banner dropped down from the top of the stalls. It said: I BET YOU CAN'T SAY THIS!

Then a deep voice came out of the boom box.

---

* It was the top hat that she put on her head. It would be weird to put a desk drawer on your head.

"Welcome to everyone's favorite
TV game show, *I Bet You Can't Say This!*
And here's your host, *Misssssssssssss* . . .
Laney!"

Wild applause came out of the boom box.

"Thank you, thank you!" said Miss Laney. "Are you kids ready to play *I Bet You Can't Say This!*?"

"Yes!" said Andrea and Emily.

"No!" said me and Ryan.

"I love game shows!" said Emily, clapping her hands excitedly.

"All righty then!" Miss Laney said. "We'll start the game in a minute. But first, this important message . . ."

Hey kids! Do you have trouble saying the letter S? When you say the word "lion," does it come out like

"wion"? Do you stutter or lisp? Don't feel bad. You're not alone. Millions of kids just like you have the same problem. But you're in luck! With the help of Miss Laney's Amazing Zany Brainy No Painy Speech Fixer Upper, you'll be able to say hard words like "February." Words like "refrigerator," "nuclear," and "duct tape." You'll be able to say EVERY WORD IN THE ENGLISH

LANGUAGE! In a few short weeks you'll be talking perfectly. It's simply amazing! But it's not available in stores. Go to www.misslaneyiszany.com and order now. Miss Laney's Amazing Zany Brainy No Painy Speech Fixer Upper is only $19.99. But wait, there's more! If you order in the next ten minutes, you'll get volume two—Miss Laney's Rainy Day No Complainy Speech Training Maintainer. It's absolutely free! Wow! What have you got to lose? All that for just $19.99. And if you're not completely satisfied, I'll refund every penny. How can I make

this crazy offer? Because Miss Laney
is . . . INSANEY! Order NOW!

You Can't Say It!

That was weird. Miss Laney did an info-mercial in the girls' bathroom!

"How many of those things have you sold so far?" Ryan asked.

"So far?" Miss Laney replied. "None."

"You'd probably sell more if you did it on TV," I suggested, "instead of in the bathroom."

"Good idea!" Miss Laney said. "Okay, welcome back to *I Bet You Can't Say This!* Our first category is tongue twisters. The winner will get a prize from the mystery treasure chest. Are you kids excited?"

"Yes!" said Andrea and Emily.

"No!" said me and Ryan.

"Let's spin the magic spinner to see who goes first!" shouted Miss Laney.

She reached into the desk and took out one of those little spinners they use for board games.

"And our first contestant is . . . A.J.!" Miss Laney said. "Okay, repeat after me—"

"After me," I repeated.

"No," Miss Laney said, "I mean, repeat what I'm about to say."

"What I'm about to say," I repeated.

"Aha-ha, very funny, A.J.," said Miss Laney. "Here's your tongue twister. 'A skunk sat on a stump. The stump thought the skunk stunk. The skunk thought the stump stunk. What stunk? The skunk or the stump?'"

I took a deep breath.

"'A skunk sat on a thunk—'"

BZZZZZZZZZZZZZZZZ!

Where did *that* come from? I didn't even see her hit a buzzer.

"Sorry! Nice try, A.J.," Miss Laney said. "But YOU CAN'T SAY IT!"

She took a kazoo out of her pocket and blew into it.

"YOU CAN'T SAY IT!" shouted Ryan, Andrea, and Emily.

"Let's spin the magic spinner to see who goes next!" said Miss Laney. "Our next contestant is . . . Emily! Repeat after me. 'A big black bug bit a big black bear. The big black bug made the big black bear bleed blood.'"

"'A big back blug—,'" Emily began.

BZZZZZZZZZZZZZZZZZ!

"Sorry! Nice try, Emily!" said Miss Laney as she blew into the kazoo. "But YOU CAN'T SAY IT!"

"YOU CAN'T SAY IT!" I shouted with Ryan and Andrea.

"Let's spin the magic spinner!" Miss Laney said. "Our next contestant is . . . Ryan! Repeat after me. 'A noisy noise annoys an oyster.'"

"'A noisy noise . . .'"

BZZZZZZZZZZZZZZZZZ!

"Oh! You took too much time!" said Miss Laney, and she blew into the kazoo. "Sorry, Ryan!"

"YOU CAN'T SAY IT!" I shouted with Andrea and Emily.

"Our last contestant in this round is Andrea," said Miss Laney. "Repeat after me. 'If Stu chews shoes, should Stu choose the shoes he chews?'"

"'If Stu chews shoes, should Stu choose the shoes he chews?'" Andrea repeated.

"Very good, Andrea!" said Miss Laney. "You win round one."

That was totally not fair. Anybody could say that thing about Stu's shoes. It's a lot harder to say my thing about the skunk.

Miss Laney said Andrea could have a smelly sticker because she won round one. There were grape, cool mint, tutti-frutti, and root beer stickers. Andrea chose grape.

"I love smelly stickers!" Andrea said.

I hate her.

We moved on to round two. I had to say "I saw a saw in Arkansas that could out saw any other saw I ever saw." Andrea had to say "Fred fed Ted bread, and Ted fed Fred bread." Ryan had to say "If two witches were watching two watches, which witch would watch which watch?" Emily had to say "I wish to wish the wish you wish to wish, but if you wish the wish the witch wishes, I won't wish the wish you wish to wish."

After three rounds I thought my tongue was gonna fall out. Miss Laney gave us water so our mouths wouldn't catch on fire.

"The judges are almost finished tabulating their results," said Miss Laney. "Today's winner is . . . Andrea!"

"Yay!" yelled Andrea.

"Congratulations," Miss Laney said. "You can take any prize you want from the mystery treasure chest."

Miss Laney opened up one of the stall doors, and there was a treasure chest inside. Andrea chose a solar-powered calculator. The rest of us were allowed to take a lollipop.

"Thanks for playing *I Bet You Can't Say This!*" Miss Laney said. "That's our show for today. You've been a *wonderful* audience. Don't forget to order your copy of Miss Laney's Amazing Zany Brainy No Painy Speech Fixer Upper! Good night, everybody!"

Cheering came out of the boom box again.

Miss Laney is weird.

Problem
Solved

The next day me and the guys were waiting in line for lunch in the vomitorium when we saw some kids nearby sobbing and crying and freaking out. They were talking with Mr. Loring, the music teacher, and Ms. Hannah, the art teacher. Both of them were carrying big cardboard boxes.

"What's going on?" asked Neil the nude kid.

"We're going home," Ms. Hannah replied. "We just got fired. We wanted to say good-bye."

"WHAT?!" I said. "I thought the school wasn't closing until June."

"That's right," said Mr. Loring. "But they're starting to fire the teachers *now*."

"Art and music are always the first to go," Ms. Hannah told us. "Some people think the arts aren't important."

"What are you gonna do now?" asked Ryan.

"I'm going to make dresses out of old pot holders and sell them on eBay," said Ms. Hannah.

"I might get back together with the guys in my old rock band and go on tour," said Mr. Loring.

It was hard to believe that Mr. Loring used to be in a rock band. He's like a million hundred years old.

"What was the name of your band?" I asked.

"The Rolling Stones," he said.

We took our trays and found seats next to Andrea and her annoying friends. They looked like they had been crying. Everybody was sad about the teachers being fired. Nobody was in the mood to eat lunch. Not even Ryan, who will eat anything, even stuff that isn't food. One time he took a bite out of the cushion on the school bus.

We were sitting there quietly when those two guys in overalls carried this big thing out of the vomitorium.

"What's *that*?" I asked.

"That's the salad bar," said Andrea.

"Is that like a candy bar made out of

salad?" I asked. Andrea rolled her eyes.

"You probably never tasted salad in your life, Arlo," she said.

"I did too," I told her. "I tasted a salad once. Then I spit it out."

"I don't care if they take away the salad bar," Michael said, "as long as they don't take away the monkey bars."

All of us looked out the window toward the playground. And you'll never believe in a million hundred years what we saw. That's right! Two guys in overalls were moving the monkey bars!

"They're taking the school apart while we're sitting here!" yelled Andrea.

"It's not fair!" yelled Ryan.

"We've got to *do* something!" yelled Emily, and then she went running out of the room.

Sheesh! Get a grip! What a crybaby!

But Emily was right for once in her life. We *did* have to do something. The question was, What?

I thought and thought and thought and thought.* I thought so hard that I thought

---

* Isn't "thought" one of those words that sounds weirder the more you say it? What's up with that?

46

my head was gonna explode. But that's when I thought of the greatest idea in the history of the world!

"Hey," I said. "Mr. Klutz told us it would take a million dollars to keep the school open, right?"

"Right," everybody said.

"So if we could get a million dollars, we could save the school!"

"A.J., you're a genius!" said Michael.

"No wonder you're in the gifted and talented program!" said Neil the nude kid.

So the solution to our problem was simple. All we had to do was get a million dollars.

How to Get a Million Dollars

6

After lunch we went outside for recess. Me and the guys went to the playground where the monkey bars used to be. Andrea, Emily, and some of their girly friends came out there too. Everybody was complaining about what was happening to our school.

"Stop whining," I told them. "All we need

to do is get a million dollars."

"How are you going to get a million dollars, Arlo?" asked Andrea. "Are you going to rob a bank?"

"Of course not!" I said. "I'll just go to the bank and get the money from the cash machine. That's what my mom does."

Andrea rolled her eyes.

"You have to put money *into* a bank if you want to take it *out*, dumbhead!" Andrea said.

"You're the dumbhead!" I told her. "What's the point of putting money in the bank if you're just gonna take it out?"

"Let's see how much money we have right now," Michael suggested.

We emptied our pockets. I had a nickel and three pennies. Ryan had a quarter. We put all the coins in a pile, and Andrea counted it.

"It comes to $1.04," she said. "And a Life-Saver."

"That's not even *close* to a million dollars," said Neil.

"Sure it is," I told him. "If we just did that a million more times, we'd have a million dollars."

"That's ridiculous, Arlo," Andrea said.

"So is your face," I told her.

"We could bake cookies," Emily suggested. "If we sold a million cookies for a dollar each, we'd make a million dollars."

"You're not gonna sell a million cookies," said Ryan.

"What if we sold just one really *big* cookie and charged a million dollars for it?" I suggested.

"Maybe we could borrow a million dollars from our parents," said Michael.

"We would have to pay it back," Andrea said. "So we would still have to get a million dollars."

"I know!" I said, snapping my fingers.

"We could clean couches."

Everybody looked at me like I was crazy. But it made perfect sense. My mom is always picking loose change out of the back of our couch. She calls it her secret couch money. We could go around town asking people if we could clean their couches and keep all the secret couch money.

"I don't think so, dude," Michael said.

"We could sell my little brother," suggested Neil the nude kid.

"That's against the law," said Andrea.

"It is not," I said.

"Is too," said Andrea.

We went back and forth like that for a

while. Suddenly, Mr. Tony came over. He's a big guy with a mustache who runs the after-school program.

"Hi, Mr. Tony!" we all said.

"What are you doing here?" asked Michael. "School doesn't let out until three o'clock."

"Because of the budget cuts," he said, "they told me I have to be on duty for recess."

We all giggled, because Mr. Tony said "on duty," which sounds exactly the same as "on doody." The weird thing is, it's okay to say "duty," but you're not supposed to say "doody." Nobody knows why. So, any time anybody says "duty," you have to giggle because it sounds like they said "doody." That's the first rule of being a kid.

Mr. Tony asked us what we were talking about, and we told him some of our ideas to get a million dollars. He gathered us around him, like we were having a football huddle.

"I have a better idea," Mr. Tony whispered. "Here's the plan. We tell the government we have a *thousand* kids at our school. Yeah, that's it. And we tell 'em our school is ten stories high. We tell 'em our school is the biggest school in the whole country."

"Why would *that* get us a million dollars?" asked Andrea.

"Simple," Mr. Tony said. "If the government thinks our school is the biggest school in the country, they'll think it's too big to fail. They'll *have* to bail us out."

We all looked at Mr. Tony.

"How can they bail us out?" I asked. "We're not boats."

Why is everybody always talking about boats? If you ask me, Mr. Tony is full of baloney.

Spooch

After recess we went back to Mr. Granite's class. He was talking about saving energy, like always. It was really boring. If you ask me, Mr. Granite should save energy by not talking so much about saving energy.

I ripped a sheet of paper out of my notebook and wrote this on it . . .

Ask if we can go see Miss Laney.

I folded my note up until it was tiny and passed it to Ryan. He looked at it and raised his hand.

"Mr. Granite," Ryan asked, "can I go to the girls' bathroom?"

Everybody laughed.

"Miss Laney will call for you if she needs to see you, Ryan," said Mr. Granite.

"Please? Please? Please? *Please?*" Ryan begged.

Any time you want something really badly, just say "please" over and over again until grown-ups can't stand it any- more. That's the first rule of being a kid.

"No, I'm sorry, Ryan," Mr. Granite said.

That's when I came up with the greatest idea in the history of the world. I raised my hand and Mr. Granite called on me.

"I need to go to spooch," I said.

"'Spooch'?" Mr. Granite asked. "What's 'spooch'?"

"You know, spooch," I told him. "That thing Miss Laney teaches."

"Do you mean 'speech,' A.J.?" Mr. Granite asked.

"Yeah," I said, "spooch."

"Why are you saying 'spooch,' A.J.?" he asked.

"I didn't say 'spooch,'" I told him. "I said 'spooch.'"

"A.J. has a spooch in president," said Ryan.

"You mean a speech impediment?" asked Mr. Granite.

"Yeah, that thing," Ryan said.

Andrea raised her hand.

"Mr. Granite," she said, "I think my

tongue is broken. Glub glub glub glub."

"Help!" yelled Emily. "I forgot how to talk!"

"I think it's contagious!" Ryan hollered. "The whole class might catch it!"

Mr. Granite looked like he was worried. I grabbed my throat and pretended to be choking. So did Ryan, Andrea, and Emily.

"It's an epidermis!" I yelled.

"You mean an epidemic?" asked Mr. Granite. "This sounds like an emergency to me! Okay, A.J., Andrea, Ryan, and Emily, I want you to go see Miss Laney right away! Hurry!"

Ha-ha! What a scam. Grown-ups will fall for anything. I knew it would be way more fun to play cool games with Miss Laney than to sit in Mr. Granite's class and learn how to save energy.

"A.J., you're a genius!" Ryan said as we walked down the hall to the girls' bathroom. "You should get the No Bell Prize for that one."

That's a prize they give out to people who don't have bells.

What's in the Stall?

When we got to the girls' bathroom, Miss Laney was combing her hair in the mirror.* She didn't notice us at first.

"Shampoo," she said to herself. "Shampoooooo. Shamp ooooo. Sham. Poo. Poo

---

* Well, her hair wasn't in the mirror. It was on her head. If her hair was in the mirror, it would be weird.

sham. *Poosh* ham. *Poo—*"

Miss Laney is weird. We started fake coughing so she would notice us.

"Oh, hello!" she said. "I was just practicing my *ooo* sounds while I fixed my hair."

"Is your hair broken?" I asked.

Everybody laughed even though I didn't say anything funny.

"To what do I owe the pleasure of your company?" Miss Laney asked us.

(That's grown-up talk for "What are *you* doing here?")

"We came to play *I Bet You Can't Say This!* again," Ryan said.

"Let's play a *different* game!" Miss Laney said as she put some weird puppet thing on her hand. "Meet Ollie the Octopus! He's your friend! He likes to play a game called *Name the Letter.*"

"How do you play?" Emily asked.

"Don't ask me!" said Miss Laney. "Ask Ollie!"

"How do you play, Ollie?" Emily asked the puppet.

"First, I tell you what to do with your mouth," Ollie said. "Then you tell me what letters you can make. For instance, what letters can you make if you push your lips together?"

I went through the alphabet silently, trying to figure out what letters I could make by pushing my lips together.

"*B* . . . *M* . . . and . . . *P*!" shouted Andrea.

"Very good!" said Ollie the Octopus. "You're winning, Andrea!"

"Yay!" shouted Andrea.

I hate her.

"Okay, next question," said Ollie. "What letters do you make when you push air through your teeth?"

I went through the alphabet in my head.

"*C* . . . and *S*!" I yelled.

"Good, A.J.!" said Ollie the Octopus. "Next question. What letters do you make by putting your tongue on the roof of your mouth?"

"*D, N,* and *T*!" I yelled.

"Right!" said Ollie. "And what letter do you make by sticking your tongue through your teeth?"

"*L*!" I shouted before anybody else. I totally rule at *Name the Letter.*

"Correct!" Ollie said. "And what letters can you make by vibrating your throat?"

"Can I phone a friend?" asked Ryan.

"*V* and *Z*!" I yelled.

"That's it!" Ollie said. "The winner is . . . A.J.!"

Andrea looked all mad. Ha-ha-ha! In her face! It was about time I won something. Nah-nah-nah boo-boo on her. It was the greatest day of my life.

Miss Laney—I mean Ollie the Octopus— said I could pick a prize from the mystery treasure chest. I chose a paddle that had a ball attached to it with a rubber band. It was cool.

"Okay, A.J.," Ollie said, "it's time to play a new game called . . . *What's in the Stall?*

You can keep that paddle, *or* you can have whatever is in Stall Number One, Stall Number Two, or Stall Number Three. It's your choice. Maybe there's a skateboard in one of the stalls. Or maybe there's a BRAND-NEW CAR!"

"You can't fit a car into a bathroom stall," Andrea said.

"It could be a very *small* car," Ryan pointed out.

"Pick Stall Number One, A.J.!" Emily yelled.

"Pick Number Three!" yelled Ryan.

"Keep the paddle, Arlo!" Andrea yelled.

I didn't know what to do. I didn't know what to say. I had to think fast. This was the hardest decision I had to make in my life. My brain hurt.

"I'll take what's in Stall Number Two," I finally said.

"Is that your final answer?" asked Ollie.

"Final answer."

Miss Laney took away my paddle and opened the door to Stall Number Two.

"Oh, sorry!" Ollie said. "You won a toilet bowl plunger. Better luck next time, A.J."

"That's not a prize!" I complained. "That thing was in the stall anyway!"

"Sorry!" Ollie said. "The decisions of the judges are final. Thanks for playing *What's in the Stall?*"

I don't like that game.

Plays Are Boring

The next day me and Ryan were walking up the front steps to school.

"Maybe Miss Laney isn't a real speech teacher," said Ryan. "Maybe she's just some crazy person who loves game shows."

"Yeah," I said, "maybe she kidnapped our real speech teacher and locked her in a grass hut on a desert island. Stuff like that happens all the time, y'know."

When we got to Mr. Granite's class, two guys in overalls were taking the whiteboard off the wall.

"What's going on?" Mr. Granite shouted.

"Sorry, pal," the guys said as they carried

the whiteboard away. "Budget cuts."

"Mr. Granite, you've got to *do* something!" Emily said.

"I don't want to rock the boat," said Mr. Granite sadly.

What *boat*?

I didn't get the chance to ask why everybody's always talking about boats, because guess who came running into the door at that moment?

Nobody, because if you ran into a door it would hurt. But guess who came running into the door*way*?

It was Miss Laney! She had a laundry bag over her shoulder.

"I just thought of how we can save the

school!" Miss Laney shouted excitedly. "We can put on a *play*! People would pay to get in. All your parents and friends would come. We could make a million dollars!"

"I love plays!" said the girls.

"I hate plays," said the boys.

"Plays are boring," I said. "Especially plays where people start singing for no reason."

"It doesn't have to be a musical," Miss Laney said. "We can put on a Shakespeare play."

"I love him!" said Andrea. "Over the summer I memorized *The Complete Works of Shakespeare*!"

What is Andrea's problem?

"Maybe the kids could do *Romeo and Juliet*," suggested Mr. Granite. "That's my favorite play."

"Great idea!" said Miss Laney.

I didn't like where this was going. Miss Laney would probably make me play Romeo. Andrea was sure to be Juliet. And then the guys would make fun of me and say I love Andrea.

"Wait a minute," I said. "Is there gonna be kissing in this play?"

"No," Miss Laney assured me. "In fact, *Romeo and Juliet* is a very violent story. At the end Juliet stabs herself and dies."

"Andrea should play Juliet," I said.

"Arlo, that's mean!" Andrea said.

"And Romeo drinks poison and dies," Mr. Granite added.

"Well, Andrea should play him too," I suggested.

"You can't have the same person play Romeo *and* Juliet!" Emily said.

"We have to hold auditions," Miss Laney said. "That will make it fair."

She dumped out her laundry bag and made us put on weird clothes with puffy shoulders that nobody in their right mind would ever wear. At least I got a sword, which was cool. Then Miss Laney passed out scripts and made us each read a line out loud.

"Good night, Good night!" Michael said.

"Parting is such sweet sorrow, That I shall say good night till it be morrow."

"What's in a name?" said Emily. "That

which we call a rose by any other name would smell as sweet."

"See, how she leans her cheek upon her hand!" said Neil the nude kid. "O that I were a glove upon that hand, That I might touch that cheek!"

After we all read a few lines, Miss Laney made her decision.

"Andrea will be Juliet, and A.J. will be Romeo," she announced.

I *knew* it!

"Oooooh!" Ryan said. "A.J. and Andrea are going to be Romeo and Juliet. They must be in *love!*"

"When are you gonna get married?" asked Michael.

If those guys weren't my best friends, I would hate them.

Miss Laney gave out the rest of the parts, and then we had to start rehearsing.

"O Romeo, Romeo!" Andrea said. "Wherefore art thou Romeo?"

"I'm right here, dumbhead," I replied.

"That's *not* the line, Arlo!" Andrea said, rolling her eyes.

We practiced the play for a long time when suddenly, guess who walked into the room?

It was Mr. Klutz!

"To what do we owe the pleasure of your company, Mr. Klutz?" asked Miss Laney.

"Did you get a million bucks to save the

school?" asked Michael.

"No," Mr. Klutz replied, "it looks like we missed the boat."

What boat? Why is everybody always talking about *boats*?!

"Do you have more bad news for us?" asked Mr. Granite.

"Yes," Mr. Klutz said sadly. "I'm very sorry to tell you this, but Miss Laney . . . you're fired."

"WHAT?!"

Everybody freaked out. Andrea collapsed on the floor and started sobbing.

"O woe! O woeful, woeful, woeful day!" she said. "Never was seen so black a day as this. O woeful day!"

A Surprise Assembly

We couldn't believe it! Miss Laney had just been hired, and now she was fired! It took us about a week to get over the shock.

Teachers were getting fired left and right that week. Mrs. Yonkers, the computer teacher, was the next to go. Then Ms. Coco, the gifted and talented teacher, got fired a few days later. Even our vice principal, Mrs. Jafee, lost her job. It was depressing saying good-bye to them all.

We were in class when Mrs. Patty announced that everybody had to go to the all-purpose room for a surprise assembly. When we got there, Mr. Klutz was up on the stage. He looked serious. Nobody was cracking jokes.

"I just wanted to say how proud I am of you kids," he told us. "You've been working very hard to raise money to save the school. But it wasn't enough. I'm very sad to tell you that today is my last day at Ella Mentry School. I just got fired."

"NO!" we all shouted.

Mr. Klutz couldn't be fired! How can you have a school with no principal? Everybody was freaking out.

That's when the most amazing thing in the history of the world happened. Mrs. Patty came running into the all-purpose room.

"Turn on the TV!" she shouted. "Turn on the TV!"

We hardly ever get to watch TV at school. The custodian, Miss Lazar, wheeled a big TV on the stage and turned it on.

"Welcome back to *Win Money or Eat Bugs*! I'm your host, Dickie Blinkbarker!"

The studio audience cheered.

"That's my favorite show!" I yelled.

The TV camera pulled back. There was a lady sitting in a chair. She had dark hair. I leaned forward to see the TV better. The lady was . . .

Miss Laney!

"Miss Laney's on TV!" we all started shrieking. "Miss Laney's on TV!"

Everybody was yelling and screaming and freaking out.

"Okay! Miss Laney won ten *thousand* dollars in round one," said Dickie Blinkbarker, "and she didn't have to eat a single bug."

"Yay!" we all shouted.

"I hear you're a speech teacher, Miss Laney, and you *love* game shows."

"Yes, Dickie," said Miss Laney, "and I want to say hi to all the kids at Ella Mentry School. That's who I'm playing for today. Every dollar I win goes directly to the school."

She waved at the camera. We waved back at the TV screen.

"That's fantastic!" said Dickie Blink-barker. "Miss Laney, you know the rules to *Win Money or Eat Bugs.* You can eat one bug at the start of round two and walk away with the ten thousand dollars you already won. Or you can keep going. But if you get a question wrong from now on, you'll lose the money you won, *and* you'll have to eat a whole *plate full of bugs.*"

"EWWWWWWWWWWWWWWW!"

everybody said when they showed a plate full of bugs.

"The questions get harder in round two," Dickie added. "So, what do you want to do?"

"Eat the bug!" some kids yelled.

"Keep going!" other kids yelled.

"I'm going to keep going, Dickie," said Miss Laney. "I want to win a million dollars."

"Miss Laney is gonna win enough money to save our school!" Michael shouted.

"YAYYYYYYYYYYYYYY!"

Mr. Klutz made the shut-up peace sign with his fingers so we could hear.

"Okay, she's going to risk it all!" said

Dickie Blinkbarker. "Here's your first question, Miss Laney. What is the longest word in the English language?"

"Oh no!" I whispered to Michael. "Nobody knows that. Miss Laney's gonna have to eat all those bugs."

"Pneumonoultramicroscopicsilicovolcanoconiosis," said Miss Laney.

"That's right!" Dickie Blinkbarker yelled. "Hardly *anybody* knows that! Miss Laney, you just won *fifty thousand dollars!*"

"YAYYYYYYYYYYYYYYYYYYYYY!"

"Next question," said Dickie Blinkbarker. "Why are manhole covers round instead of square?"

I had no idea why manhole covers were

round. I was sure Miss Laney would get it wrong and have to eat a plate full of bugs.

"Square manhole covers could fall into a manhole," said Miss Laney. "Round ones can't."

"That's right!" shouted Dickie Blinkbarker. "Miss Laney, you just won *one hundred thousand dollars!*"

"YAYYYYYYYYYYYYYYYYYYYY!"

"She's gonna win a million! She's gonna win a million!"

Everybody was jumping up and down and hugging each other. You should have been there!

"Okay, here's your final question, Miss

Laney," said Dickie Blinkbarker. "This would put you over the top. For one *million* dollars—what is the science of sound called?"

"A cue stick!" I yelled.

"Acoustics!" yelled Andrea. "Miss Laney is going to win a million dollars!"

"Uh . . . ," said Miss Laney.

"Acoustics!" everybody screamed as if Miss Laney could hear us through the TV.

"Uh . . . uh . . ."

"She doesn't remember!" I groaned, slapping my head.

"Uh . . . uh . . . uh . . ."

"She's got brain freeze!" groaned Ryan.

"Gee!" said Dickie Blinkbarker. "I never heard of a speech teacher who was speechless!"

"I know the answer," said Miss Laney frantically. "It's on the tip of my tongue."

BZZZZZZZZZZZZZZZZZZ!

"Ohhhhhhhhhhh!" everybody groaned.

"I'm *soooooo* sorry, Miss Laney," said Dickie Blinkbarker. "The correct answer is 'acoustics.' Speaking of the tip of your tongue, bring out the bugs!"

Ugh, Disgusting!

We all watched the TV. Some lady wearing a bathing suit came out carrying a plate. The camera zoomed in for a close-up, and you could see all these disgusting bugs slithering around on it. I thought I was gonna throw up.

This had to be the saddest day in the history of the world. Miss Laney didn't win a million dollars. She didn't save the school. And now she would have to eat a plate full of bugs. Some of the first graders were crying.

"Eat bugs! Eat bugs!" the studio audience chanted.

"Before you eat the bugs," said Dickie Blinkbarker, "is there anything you'd like to say to the folks out there in TV land, Miss Laney?"

"Yes, there is, Dickie," Miss Laney said. She turned to face the camera, and it moved in for a close-up.

Hey kids! Do you have trouble saying the letter S? When you say the word 'lion,' does it come out like 'wion'? Do you

stutter or lisp? Don't feel bad. You're not alone. Millions of kids just like you have the same problem. But you're in luck! With the help of Miss Laney's Amazing Zany Brainy No Painy Speech Fixer Upper, you'll be able to say hard words like 'February.' Words like 'refrigerator,' 'nuclear,' and 'duct tape.' You'll be able

to say **EVERY WORD IN THE ENGLISH LANGUAGE! In a few short weeks, you'll be talking perfectly. It's simply amazing! But it's not available in stores. Go to www.misslaneyiszany.com and order now. Miss Laney's Amazing Zany Brainy No Painy Speech Fixer Upper is only $19.99. But wait, there's more!**

Miss Laney did her whole infomercial on national TV!

"I'm going to go check Miss Laney's website!" Mrs. Patty yelled. She ran to the front office, which is next to the all-purpose room.

On TV, Miss Laney finished her infomercial. Then she picked up a spider and ate it.

"EWWWWWWWWWWWWWWW!" we all screamed.

"Orders are pouring in like crazy!" Mrs. Patty shouted from the front office.

On TV, Miss Laney ate an ant.

"EWWWWWWWWWWWWWWW!" we all screamed.

"So far there are twenty thousand dollars' worth of orders!" shouted Mrs. Patty.

On TV, Miss Laney ate some flies.

"EWWWWW-WWWWWWWWW!" we all screamed.

"Fifty thousand dollars in orders so far!" shouted Mrs. Patty.

On TV, Miss Laney ate a beetle.

"EWWWWWWWWWWWWW!" we all screamed.

"It's up to a hundred thousand dollars!" shouted Mrs. Patty.

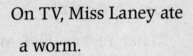

On TV, Miss Laney ate a worm.

"EWWWWWW-WWWWWWWW-WWWWWWWW!" we all screamed.

"A half a million dollars!" shouted Mrs. Patty.

On TV, Miss Laney ate a cockroach.

"EWWWWWWWWW-
WWWWW!" we all
screamed.

"A *million dollars*!"
shouted Mrs. Patty.
"She sold a million
dollars' worth of her
speech program!"

"That means Ella Mentry School can
stay open!" I hollered. "Miss Laney saved
the school!"

Everybody was yelling and screaming and jumping up and down and going
crazy. On TV, Miss Laney finished all the
bugs on the plate.

"You've been a good sport, Miss Laney,"

said Dickie Blinkbarker. "Even though you didn't win, here's a check for a thousand dollars just for playing *Win Money or Eat Bugs*."

"Thank you, Dickie," said Miss Laney.

"But we're not done yet!" Dickie said. "You can keep the money, *or* you can have what's behind the curtain!"

The lady in the bathing suit stood in front of the curtain.

"Take the money!" some kids shouted.

"Pick the curtain!" other kids shouted.

"I'll take what's behind the curtain, Dickie," said Miss Laney.

"Okay, let's see what she won!" said Dickie Blinkbarker.

The curtain opened, and you'll never believe in a million hundred years what was behind it.

I'm not gonna tell you.

Okay, okay, I'll tell you.

It was a *boat*!

Dickie Blinkbarker and Miss Laney climbed into the boat and pretended to row it even though there wasn't any water.

"We're on a boat!" they said.

It was hilarious.

So, to make a long story short, our school doesn't have to close after all. Maybe all the teachers who got fired will get their

jobs back. Maybe Mr. Granite will get his desk and whiteboard back. Maybe they'll put back the salad bar and the monkey bars. Maybe Miss Laney will get a regular office instead of a bathroom. Maybe it will have a pool table in it so she can get some good cue sticks. Maybe Miss Laney will give us a ride in her new boat. Maybe Mr. Klutz will grow some hair. Maybe I can go to speech class every day. Maybe I'll figure out why everybody is always talking about boats for no reason.

But it won't be easy!